CONTENTS

Any words appearing in the text in bold, **like this**, are explained in the glossary. You can also look out for them in the **On the rocks!** section at the bottom of each page.

FASCINATING FOSSILS

Some rocks can tell us about life in the past. These rocks contain the remains of ancient plants and animals. We call these remains fossils.

Fossils come in all shapes and sizes. Huge dinosaur fossils have been found in some rocks. This is how we know that dinosaurs once lived on Earth. Other fossils are too tiny for our eyes to see.

Oldest fossils
The oldest fossils ever found are **algae**. These are tiny plants. Scientists think that this is how life on Earth began.

⇩ **This is Dinosaur National Monument, in the United States. Large dinosaur fossils have been found here.**

Geology Rocks!

ssils

EXPRESS EDITION

Raintree

www.raintreepublishers.co.uk
Visit our website to find out more information about **Raintree** books.

To order:
☎ Phone 44 (0) 1865 888112
🗎 Send a fax to 44 (0) 1865 314091
💻 Visit the Raintree bookshop at **www.raintreepublishers.co.uk** to browse our catalogue and order online.

First published in Great Britain by Raintree,
Halley Court, Jordan Hill, Oxford OX2 8EJ,
part of Harcourt Education.
Raintree is a registered trademark
of Harcourt Education Ltd.

Editorial: Kathryn Walker, Melanie Waldron and
Rachel Howells
Design: Victoria Bevan, Rob Norridge,
and AMR Design Ltd (www.amrdesign.com)
Illustrations: David Woodroffe
Picture Research: Melissa Allison and Mica Brancic
Production: Duncan Gilbert
Originated by Chroma Graphics Pte. Ltd
Printed and bound in China by
South China Printing Company

ISBN 978 1406 20902 0 (hardback)
12 11 10 09 08
10 9 8 7 6 5 4 3 2 1

ISBN 978 1406 20910 5 (paperback)
12 11 10 09 08
10 9 8 7 6 5 4 3 2 1

**British Library Cataloguing in
Publication Data**
Faulkner, Rebecca.
  Fossils. – (Geology Rocks!)
  560
A full catalogue record for this book is available
from the British Library.

This levelled text is a version of *Freestyle:
Geology Rocks: Fossils*

Acknowledgements
The publishers would like to thank the following for
permission to reproduce photographs:

©Alamy p. **14** (Phil Degginger); ©Corbis p. **17**
(Bettman); ©GeoScience Features Picture Library
pp. **10, 18, 35** (D. Bayliss), pp. **6, 21** (Martin Land),
pp. **5 top inset, 5 middle inset, 11 right, 23, 25,
33, 34 right, 42, 43** (Prof. B. Booth); ©Getty Images
p. **4** (Science Faction); ©Lonely Planet Images p. **11
left** (Richard Cummins); ©Science Photo Library p. **7**
(Alan Sirulnikoff), p. **27 bottom** (Alexis Rosenfeld),
p. **29** (Bernhard Edmaier), p. **32** (David R. Frazier),
p. **12** (Dirk Wiersma), p. **28** (Herve Conge, ISM),
p. **26 top** (Jim Amos), p. **15** (Marie Perennou and
De Nuridsany), p. **37** (Martin Bond), pp. **5, 24, 27
top** (Martin Land), p. **16** (Noah Poritz), p. **20** (Simon
Fraser), pp. **13, 22, 26 bottom, 34 left, 36, 38, 39,
44** (Sinclair Stammers); ©Still Pictures pp. **5 bottom
inset, 30** (UNEP/S. Compoint)

Cover photograph of ammonite fossils reproduced
with permission of ©Getty Images (Photonica).

Every effort has been made to contact copyright
holders of any material reproduced in this book.
Any omissions will be rectified in subsequent
printings if notice is given to the publishers.

Disclaimer
All the Internet addresses (URLs) given in this book
were valid at the time of going to press. However,
due to the dynamic nature of the Internet, some
addresses may have changed, or sites may have
changed or ceased to exist since publication. While
the author and publishers regret any inconvenience
this may cause readers, no responsibility for any
such changes can be accepted by either the author
or the publishers.

Most fossils are animals and plants that lived in the ocean. This is because these animals and plants sink to the bottom of the ocean when they die. They become buried in mud. No wind or rain can damage them there. There are few animals to disturb them.

Over time these dead plants and animals will be buried deeper and deeper. They will become fossils.

This is an ancient animal called a brachiopod. All its soft parts have disappeared. Bits of its hard shell are also missing.

Earth's moving crust

Most fossils are of animals that lived in the ocean. So why are their fossils found on land today?

This is because Earth's surface is moving all the time. The oceans are always changing in size. To understand how this happens we need to think about what is below us.

Earth is made up of layers. The **crust** is like its skin. This is where we live. Under the crust is the **mantle**. This layer is 2,900 kilometres (1,800 miles) thick.

Melting rocks
Temperatures in the mantle are very hot. Therefore the rocks there are very hot. In places they are partly melted.

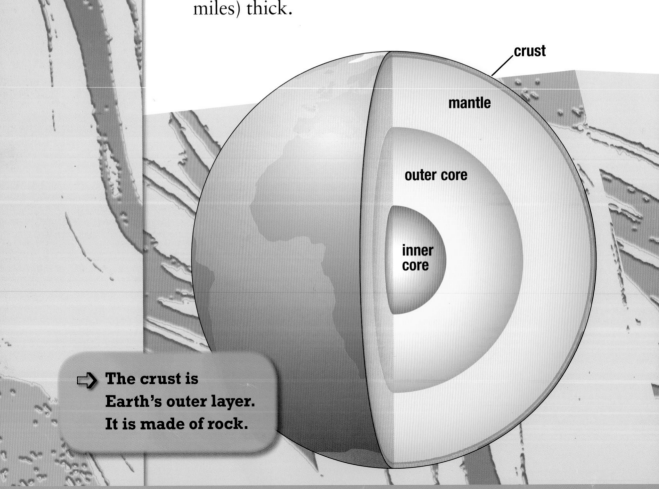

crust

mantle

outer core

inner core

⇨ **The crust is Earth's outer layer. It is made of rock.**

The **core** is the centre of Earth. There is a solid inner core and a liquid outer core. The inner core is made of hard metal. The outer core is melted metal.

Earth's crust is not one solid layer. It is broken up into huge moving pieces. These are called **plates**. They fit together like a giant jigsaw puzzle.

The plates float on Earth's mantle. They move very slowly over Earth.

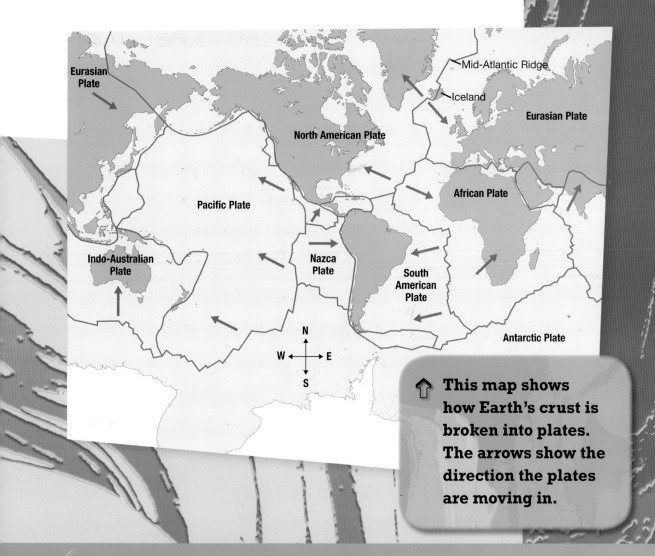

Mid-Atlantic Ridge

Iceland

Eurasian Plate

Eurasian Plate

North American Plate

Pacific Plate

African Plate

Indo-Australian Plate

Nazca Plate

South American Plate

Antarctic Plate

N
W ← → E
S

⇧ **This map shows how Earth's crust is broken into plates. The arrows show the direction the plates are moving in.**

plate giant, moving piece of the Earth's crust

Crashing plates

Sometimes Earth's **plates** (see page 9) crash into one another. Earth's **crust** (top layer) is then squashed between the plates. It is pushed up. This forms mountain ranges.

Any ocean between the plates drains away. Material from the ocean floor is also pushed up. This is why we find fossils of sea creatures in high mountains.

Changing continents

There are seven large pieces of land on Earth. These are called **continents**. They are separated by oceans. But the same fossils are found on different continents. These fossils tell us that all the continents were once joined.

Fossil detectives
People who study fossils are called **palaeontologists**. They look at fossils to find out what happened on Earth in the past.

⇩ **Fossils like this have been found in southern Africa and South America.**

Sedimentary rocks

Sedimentary rocks are formed from bits of other rocks. Rain or wind breaks off tiny pieces of rock. Wind or rivers carry them to a new place. The pieces pile up to form sedimentary rock.

Metamorphic rocks

Metamorphic rocks are rocks that have changed. Rising magma heats up the surrounding rocks. Movements in Earth's crust squash and fold rocks. This heating and squashing changes rocks. They change into metamorphic rocks.

Odd shapes
The picture below shows a fossil in metamorphic rock. Fossils in this type of rock are often out of shape. This is because of heating and squashing.

mantle   hot layer of the Earth beneath the crust

WHERE CAN WE FIND FOSSILS?

Most fossils are found in **sedimentary rocks** (see page 13). Some sedimentary rocks are made almost entirely of fossils. Chalk is one of these rocks.

Amazing fossil finds

In some parts of the world you can find amazing fossils. There are rocks that contain thousands of different types of fossils.

Fewer fossils

Very few fossils are found in **igneous** and **metamorphic rocks** (see pages 12 and 13). They are often destroyed by heating and squashing.

⇨ Wonderful fossils like this can give us lots of information about the past.

sedimentary rock rock formed from the broken pieces of other rocks

Fossils of the soft parts of animals and plants are very rare. But lots of soft-bodied fossils have been found in the Burgess shale. This is a layer of rocks in British Columbia, Canada.

About 500 million years ago the area was buried in moving mud. Animals were trapped in the mud. The mud hardened to form the rock shale. There was no time for their soft parts to rot away. The plants and animals became soft-bodied fossils.

Solnhofen limestone
The Solnhofen limestone region is in the country of Germany. The limestone rock there contains rare soft-bodied fossils. This dragonfly is one of the fossils found there.

metamorphic rock rock formed when igneous or sedimentary rocks are changed by heat or pressure

Sticky fossils

Not all fossils are found in rocks. Some are found in ice. Others are found in sticky substances such as amber and tar.

Amber fossils

Amber is a yellow-orange material. It began as a runny and sticky fluid. The fluid came from ancient

Amber jewellery
Amber has a beautiful yellow-orange colour. It is often used in jewellery.

⬇ These insects lived millions of years ago. They became trapped in amber.

amber sticky, sugary sap from ancient trees that has hardened

Sediment builds up in flat layers. These are called **beds**. Over millions of years the beds become squashed. This happens as new sediment piles on top. The grains (tiny pieces) of sediment stick together. This is how sedimentary rock forms.

Millions of years later the rocks above are worn away. This brings ancient fossils to the surface.

⬇ **Loose sediment becomes pressed and stuck together. It forms hard rock. Dead plants or animals that get into the mix will become part of the rock.**

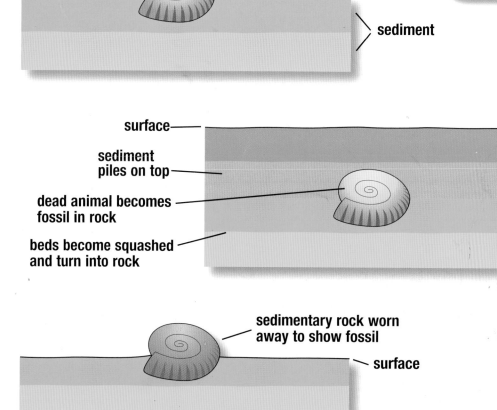

dead animal

surface

sediment

surface

sediment piles on top

dead animal becomes fossil in rock

beds become squashed and turn into rock

sedimentary rock worn away to show fossil

surface

Changes after death

Sometimes fossils are found of plants and animals just as they were in life. Some still have the soft parts. But most plants and animals change after they die. Many different changes take place.

Petrification

> ⬇ **These are the petrified remains of trees. Minerals have replaced the wood in the trees.**

A plant or animal may actually be turned to stone. This is called **petrification**. It happens because water gets into a fossil. This water contains **minerals**. Minerals are the natural materials that make up rocks.

The dead plant or animal may completely dissolve away. It breaks down and mixes with the water. Minerals from the water replace the plant or animal body. The minerals form a stone copy of it.

Moulds

Fossils are often found as **moulds** or shapes in rock. This is like the mould your footprint makes in soft mud. It happens when an animal or a shell dissolves away. It leaves a mould of itself in the rock.

Casts

Sometimes a mould becomes filled with minerals. The minerals take the shape of the mould. This is called a **cast**.

⬇ Here an animal has rotted away. It left a mould in the rock. The mould is at the bottom of picture. The cast is at the top of the picture.

mould shape or imprint left by a plant or animal in rock

COMMON FOSSILS

There are more than a million different types of fossil. They can be put into several different groups.

Brachiopods

Brachiopods live on the ocean floor. Brachiopods are very common fossils. They are found in **sedimentary rocks** (see page 13). They have two shells. One of these is longer than the other. Some types of brachiopod still exist today.

⬇ **These fossils are the shells of brachiopods.**

sedimentary rock   rock formed from the broken pieces of other rocks

Molluscs

Molluscs are animals that usually have shells. They live in water and on land. There are many types of mollusc alive today. Snails are a type of mollusc. So are mussels and cockles. But some molluscs have no shell. These include octopuses and squid.

Mollusc shells are often found as fossils. This is because they are tough. They can last a long time.

Ammonites
This picture shows an ammonite fossil. Ammonites are common mollusc fossils. They had hard, spiral-shaped shells. No ammonites exist today.

Graptolites

Graptolites used to live in the ocean. They are **extinct**. This means that no graptolites exist today.

Graptolites had tough skeletons. These are often found as fossils. Graptolite fossils are long and thin. They look like pencil markings on the rocks.

These look like pencil lines drawn on the rock. But they are the remains of graptolites.

extinct   no longer alive. A plant or animal becomes extinct when no more of its species (type) are left alive.

Trilobites

Trilobites were also sea-living animals. They too are extinct. There were once thousands of types of trilobites. They were common all over the world.

Trilobite bodies are made up of many sections. They had hard skeletons on the outside of their bodies.

⇩ **This is a trilobite. It lived in the ocean millions of years ago.**

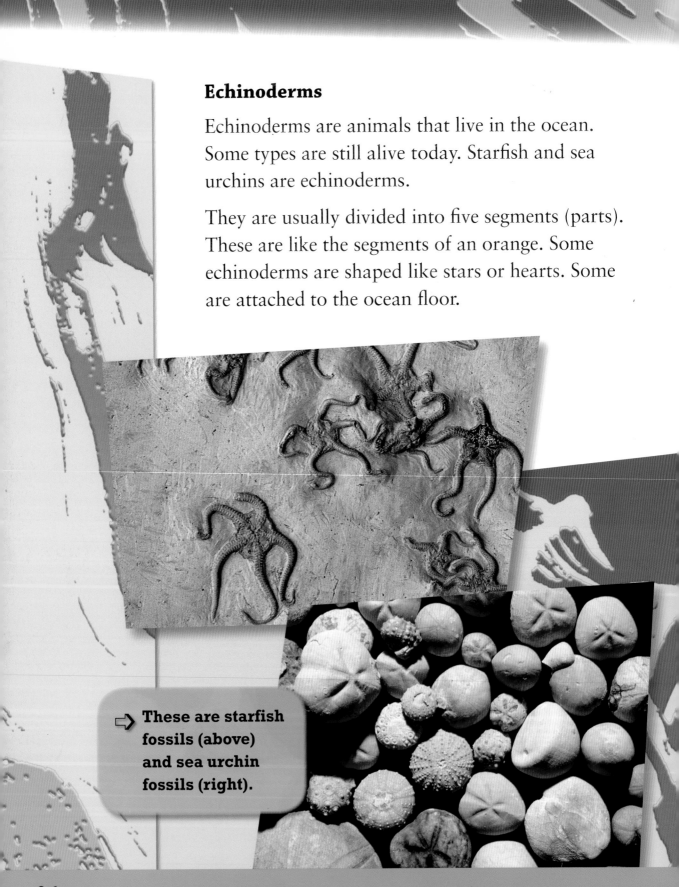

Echinoderms

Echinoderms are animals that live in the ocean. Some types are still alive today. Starfish and sea urchins are echinoderms.

They are usually divided into five segments (parts). These are like the segments of an orange. Some echinoderms are shaped like stars or hearts. Some are attached to the ocean floor.

⇨ **These are starfish fossils (above) and sea urchin fossils (right).**

common plant fossils. This is because they often have hard skeletons.

Fossils of trees can also be found. Some of these fossils are of pine and fir trees. It is usually only the woody parts of the trees that are **fossilised**. But some amazing fossils of leaves and petals have been found.

Petrified Forest
The Petrified Forest is in the state of Arizona, USA. The wood in the trees has been replaced with **minerals** (see page 20). Over millions of years the wood has petrified (turned into stone).

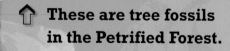
⇧ These are tree fossils in the Petrified Forest.

Turning fossils into fuels

Sedimentary rocks are made up of pieces of other rocks. They contain fossils. They also contain **fossil fuels**. Fuels are materials we burn to produce heat or power.

Oil and coal are fossil fuels. We use them to heat and light our homes. We use them to power our cars.

⬇ **These men are trying to stop the oil gushing out of an oil well. This is in the country of Kuwait.**

fossil fuel   fuel, such as coal or oil, that is made from the remains of plants and animals found in rock

Oil forms from dead plants and animals. These are remains that settled on the ocean floor. Over millions of years, they became covered by layers of **sediment** (see page 19). The remains became squashed. They turned into oil.

Coal formed from the remains of huge forests. Millions of years ago, dead forest plants and trees fell to the swampy floor. They became buried under layers of sediment. The squashed remains turned into coal.

⬇ **Coal formed from the dead remains of ancient plants.**

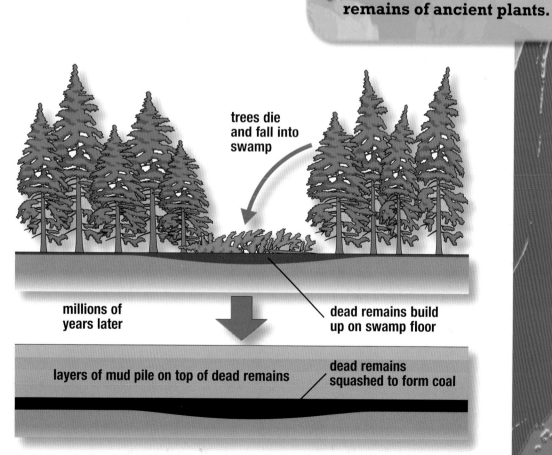

trees die and fall into swamp

millions of years later

dead remains build up on swamp floor

layers of mud pile on top of dead remains

dead remains squashed to form coal

sediment pieces of rock that have been worn away and moved to another place

CLUES LEFT BEHIND

Some of the most exciting fossils are the bones of dinosaurs. Dinosaur fossils are very rare. But some amazing fossils have been found.

The death of the dinosaurs

Palaeontologists are scientists who study fossils. They can put dinosaur bones back together. This way they can build a dinosaur's skeleton.

Scientists think that there were at least 350 different kinds of dinosaur. Some were bigger than a house. Others were as small as a chicken.

T rex

Tyrannosaurus rex (*T rex*) was a type of dinosaur. Scientists think that the *T rex* was up to 12 metres (40 feet) long from head to tail.

⬇ This is a *T rex* skeleton. Paleontologists have used fossil bones to work out what a dinosaur may have looked like.

The dinosaurs became **extinct** (died out) 65 million years ago. Fossils suggest that they were killed off by a disastrous event.

This event might have been a huge volcano exploding. It might have been a great change in weather conditions. It might have been a large meteorite hitting Earth. A meteorite is a rock that has come from space. It crashes onto Earth as a ball of fire.

Dinosaurs in the rocks
The Dinosaur National Monument stretches across the states of Utah and Colorado, USA. The rocks there contain amazing dinosaur fossils. You can see some of them in this picture.

extinct   no longer alive. A plant or animal becomes extinct when no more of its species (type) are left alive.

Traces of the past

Trace fossils are marks left in rocks by plants or animals. They may be footprints or holes. These markings can tell us how ancient animals lived.

Dinosaur footprints have been found in many parts of the world. These tell us how big the dinosaur was. They also tell us how fast it could run.

Animal droppings are another type of trace fossil. These ancient droppings are called **coprolites**.

⬆ This is a fossil dropping. It came from a turtle.

⇨ A dinosaur made this footprint. It became a fossil.

Some coprolites contain shells or bones. Some contain fish scales. This gives us information about what ancient animals ate.

Fossils of eggs of ancient animals have been found. These give clues about the size of the animal that laid them. Sometimes scientists have been able to cut open an egg fossil. They have found a fossil of the growing animal inside.

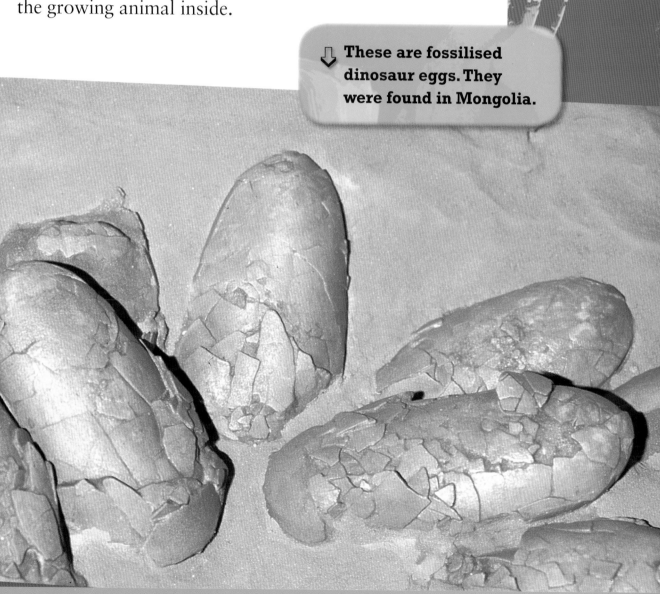

⇩ These are fossilised dinosaur eggs. They were found in Mongolia.

coprolite   ancient animal droppings

BECOME A PALAEONTOLOGIST

Fossils tell us about life in the past. They are the only way we know about dinosaurs. They have also told us about plants and other animals that lived millions of years ago.

Evidence from fossils

Fossils show that life began on Earth more than 2 billion years ago. Since then many plants and animals have become **extinct**. They no longer exist. Only a few have survived as fossils.

Vanished!

Fossils do not tell us everything about life in the past. There are lots of plants and animals we know nothing about. This is because there are no traces of them left.

➡ **This starfish lived 55 million years ago.**

36   **On the rocks!**   evolution   the process of plants and animals changing over time. They adapt to their changing surroundings.

By studying these fossils we can see that plants and animals changed over time. They changed to suit their surroundings. This process is called **evolution**.

Fossils can also tell us about changes in Earth's **climate** (weather conditions). Different plants and animals live in different climates. Studying fossils can show us how the climate of a place has changed.

⬇ **These cliffs are made from chalk. Chalk is made up of the shells of ocean creatures. This means that the area was once underwater.**

From ocean to land
Fossils of ocean animals are often found on land. This tells us that the area may have been covered with water in the past.

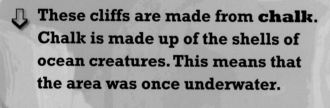

Telling the time with fossils

Scientists have gathered lots of information from fossils. They have put all the information together. This is called the **fossil record**. It tells us how life has changed over many millions of years.

We know that some animals lived at a certain time in history. If fossils of these animals are found in rock, we can work out how old that rock is.

Some animals **evolved** (changed) more quickly than others. Fossils of these animals are very useful for telling the

⬇ **This is sedimentary rock** (see page 13). Its lower layers formed before its upper layers. The fossils in the lower layers will be older than those nearer the top.

age of rocks. The changes in the animals mark smaller time periods.

Ammonites are useful for telling time. These creatures evolved quickly. Each type of ammonite lived in a different time period. This means that each type can be given an age. Then the rock can also be given an age.

Zonal fossils
The fossils in the picture below are ammonites. They are often used for telling the time period. Fossils that can be used like this are called zonal fossils.

evolve   change over time. Plants and animals evolve as they adapt to their surroundings.

The geologic timescale

Scientists have gathered lots of information from fossils. They have used it to divide up the history of Earth. This is called the **geologic timescale**. It is divided into stages called eras. Each era is made up of shorter stages called periods.

The chart below shows the geologic timescale. Look across the columns. You will see that dinosaurs lived during the Mesozoic era.

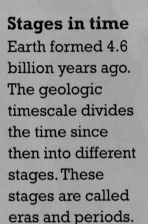

Stages in time
Earth formed 4.6 billion years ago. The geologic timescale divides the time since then into different stages. These stages are called eras and periods.

Time (millions of years ago)	Era	Period
1.8 to present	Cenozoic	Quaternary
65.5 to 1.8		Tertiary
145.5 to 65.5	Mesozoic	Cretaceous
199.6 to 145.5		Jurassic
251 to 199.6		Triassic
299 to 199.6	Palaeozoic	Permian
359.2 to 299		Carboniferous
416 to 359.2		Devonian
443.7 to 416		Silurian
488.3 to 443.7		Ordovician
542 to 488.3		Cambrian

geologic timescale way of dividing up the history of the Earth into time periods

The Mesozoic era was between 65.5 and 251 million years ago.

Dinosaurs died out at the end of the Cretaceous period. Then the mammals took over. Mammals are the group of animals that feed their young with their milk. Humans belong to this group.

Fossils of humans first appeared in the Quaternary period. This is the latest stage of the geologic timescale.

⇩ **This chart shows the geological timescale. The different stages are marked by the plants and animals that lived at that time. We are living in the Quaternary period.**

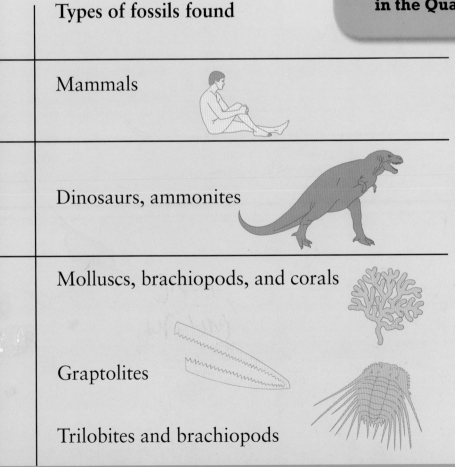

Types of fossils found
Mammals
Dinosaurs, ammonites
Molluscs, brachiopods, and corals
Graptolites
Trilobites and brachiopods

Finding your own fossils

You can find fossils anywhere in the world. You can find them in **sedimentary rocks** (see page 13). Start by looking in your own garden or in a park.

A good place to hunt for fossils is on the beach. You will need to be patient. Some days you may find nothing. But you might find a fossil that has never been seen before.

Fossil hunting

There may be a local club you can join for fossil hunting. They will organise trips. These will take you to places where you are likely to find fossils.

⬇ **You will need some equipment to go fossil hunting. Here are some of the tools scientists use to go fossil hunting.**

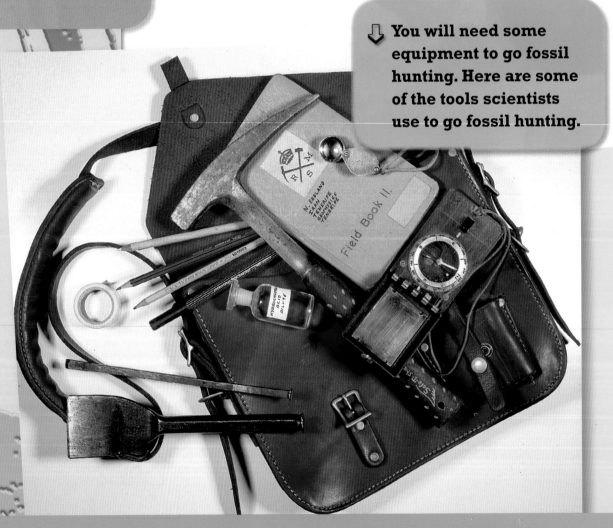

Once you have found a fossil you need to identify it. You will need to look in books. Look at pictures of all the different types of fossils. See if you can match yours to a name.

Important find
A three-year-old boy discovered pieces of dinosaur egg. These were the first to be found in the state of New Mexico, USA.

← You can look for fossils anywhere there are rocks. But you need to be very careful. All these people are wearing helmets. Helmets help to protect them from falling rocks.

SUMMARY

- Fossils are the dead remains of ancient animals and plants. The marks that plants and animals have left in rocks are also fossils. These may be footprints or holes.

- Most fossils are found in **sedimentary rocks** (see page 13).

- It is usually only the hard parts of ancient plants and animals that survive as fossils. Most fossils are of creatures that lived in the ocean.

- Fossils tell us how life on Earth has changed. Fossils are the only way we know about plants and animals that lived millions of years ago.

⟹ **These fossils are called belemnites. They were parts of sea animals similar to squid.**

FIND OUT MORE

Books

DK Eyewitness Guides: Fossil, Paul D. Taylor (Dorling Kindersley, 2003)

Energy Essentials: Fossil Fuels, Nigel Saunders and Steven Chapman (Raintree, 2005)

Fossils, Rona Arato (Crabtree Publishing Company, 2004)

Rocks and Minerals: Fossils, Melissa Stewart (Heinemann, 2003)

Using the Internet

If you want to find out more about fossils you can search the Internet. Try using keywords such as these:

- dinosaurs
- geologic timescale
- coprolites.

You can also use different keywords. Try choosing some words from this book.

Try using a search directory such as www.yahooligans.com

Search tips

There are billions of pages on the Internet. It can be difficult to find what you are looking for. These search skills will help you find useful websites more quickly:

- Know exactly what you want to find out about.
- Use two to six keywords in a search. Put the most important words first.
- Only use names of people, places, or things.

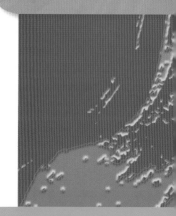

GLOSSARY

algae tiny plants

amber sticky, sugary sap from ancient trees that has hardened

bed layer of sediment

cast fossil formed when minerals get into the mould of a plant or animal

chalk sedimentary rock made from the shells of tiny ocean-living organisms

climate normal weather conditions of an area

continent one of the world's seven large landmasses

coprolite ancient animal droppings

core centre of the Earth

crust thin surface layer of Earth

deposited weathered rock laid down in a new place

evolution the process of plants and animals changing over time. They adapt to their changing surroundings.

evolve change over time. Plants and animals evolve as they adapt to their surroundings.

extinct no longer alive. A plant or animal becomes extinct when no more of its species (type) are left alive.

fossil fuel fuel, such as coal or oil, that is made from the remains of plants and animals found in rock

fossil record record of life on the Earth obtained from fossil evidence

fossilise change into a fossil

geologic timescale way of dividing up the history of the Earth into time periods

Gondwanaland ancient continent made up of South America, Africa, India, Antarctica, and Australia

igneous rock rock formed from magma either underground or at the Earth's surface

Laurasia ancient continent made up of North America, Europe, and Asia

magma melted rock from inside the Earth

mantle hot layer of the Earth beneath the crust

metamorphic rock rock formed when igneous or sedimentary rocks are changed by heat or pressure

mineral substance found in nature. Rocks are made from lots of minerals.

mould shape or imprint left by a plant or animal in rock

palaeontologist scientist who studies fossils

Pangaea ancient supercontinent, when all the present-day continents were joined together as one landmass

petrification turned to stone

plate giant, moving piece of the Earth's crust

sediment pieces of rock that have been worn away and moved to another place

sedimentary rock rock formed from the broken pieces of other rocks

trace fossil mark left in rocks by ancient plants or animals

Index

48